THE SHATTERED

G. HARSHITH

CONTENTS

*To my friend, without whom this
book wouldn' exist.*

JADE
THE WIDOW FOREST
HEAVE
SOLS
CORTIS
YANG
YIN
YIYANG
TRICKS

Prologue

The city was set ablaze. Houses were being burnt. The once so calm and dark night has been turned into a day in hell.

The House of tricks had it coming. First they had invaded Yiang and now had aimed for Sols. But they wouldn't back down, No.

The king wiped out the forces of the Tricks and marched toward the City.

Now, the city is being ruined. Families and land destroyed. Even the king of Tricks had to pay, with his life and family for what he had done.

Now even in the midst of terror. One survived.

The King's men marched forward on their horses. Travelling the road and setting each house on fire.

First they locked the doors and poured oil and finally set fire with a torch, with no concern for the people who were locked inside.

With the steady march, new houses were burned to ashes.

One particular house, the cries inside started as the fire rampaged the building.

Minutes had passed and the cry still continued. The crying of a baby was heard.

"Sir, survivors!" Said one of the soldiers, pointing to the house where he still heard the cries.

The king got down off his horse and began walking to the house. His every stride signaled power in his position.

The heat grew more, but the cries never ended.

The king put his shoulder to the door and gave one swift movement and the door came breaking down.

He entered the house filled with fires.. He covered his nose with his hand and began to move steadily. The fires didn't seem a big deal to him as he walked right through them.

His leg hit something. It was a large beam fallen from the ceiling. He put his hand under the beam and threw it over. He continued to walk in the direction of the cries. Getting louder and louder.

Until he could see a carriage which was burning. Inside there was a baby crying to the fires.

Although the fire engulfed the carriage, the baby remained unharmed. The king could sense the magic lying deep in him, with his grey hair and a tiny little face.

The King held the boy in his arms and cuddled the boy, making him laugh.

The boy held a small cloth which had the name embroidered on it.

The king looked at the name and whispered to the boy "Hax.

CHAPTER 1

I tried holding the sword with my slippery hands. The humidity of the night made my palms sweat like crazy. I tried to swing it carefully so it wouldn't hit me. The sword was twice as large as me. I was young, feeble and weak. It was very heavy.

I swung it right and left on the dummy in front, then it slipped from my hands and hit the ground with a loud clatter.

"Weak. Come on, pick it up again." Myfather commanded.I

rushed to pick it up. I saw the blade shining as it reflected the moon light coming in from the skylight of the courtyard.

"Hurry up. Time is essential in fights." I put my hand over the hilt of the blade and grab ahold of it. I take my stance once again and prepare myself. I wipe the sweat on my palms on the side of my night trousers. I hold the hilt tight and firm and position it in front of my face and look towards Father .

The moonlight glares on his silhouette making his face black. The stars illuminate the sky. Sometimes I wonder why Father made Hax, my brother a general and not me. We are the same age, twins. Maybe I didn't have it in me, hence this training session.

Maybe I am weaker than Hax. Maybe he needed brute force to rule his kingdom rather than wiseful thinking or stronger magic. Because from what I had learned that people always bow to fear. They obey the rules it makes, allow it to control their lives. Magic and sorcery were unreliable and only in a few of the people. So, fear is an effective weapon.

But I can be more, I can be better, better than Hax. That is why I need to prove myself.

I look back down and take in a deep breath and exhale.

You've got this Azen.

I say to myself. And wait for his command. "Now.'

I throw slashes and hits and jabs to the dummy in front of me. The sword tore open new cuts on the dummy. I focus all my attention on my strikes making them powerful. But, I forgot to pay attention to what was happening near me. When I had swinged once, the blade nicked my thumb exposing the bone.

I cry out a hiss and drop the blade to the ground with a loud clatter, again. "You're sloppy Azen." spits out my Father.

I argue and say "It's just–".

"No, Maybe you are not ready." He gives out a long sigh, disappointed in me. "Tomorrow, we will train again and this time make no mistakes."

But.

I kill the word in my throat. Because it isn't going to end well if I try to argue with the Cortian King.

"Fine." I also sighed. "Remember, you are a Cortian Prince." Father reminded me. He continued "Even if you aren't, you're still *My boy, My blood*. Remember that. Now, go to sleep."

Father turned the other way and headed to sleep. I was still in the courtyard with the moonlight shining through. The courtyard of the building had huge trees and wonderful and amazing plants. I walked here and there trying to get sleepy, but no. I wanted to practice, I wanted to perfect the art of fighting. So, I can finally prove that I am better than Hax.

So, I went back to the dummy and continued to throw slashes at it with the sword. Each swing made my cut burn more. And with each swing I winced to the pain.

I let the pain hit me deep, because that's what made me stronger. Because it reminded me how weak I was. It drove me to keep fighting and training.

But, it was too much for my friglie body. I was only fourteen and had just learned to pick up a sword. The pain was so excruciating that it seeped into my forearm. I grunted with every swing. I wanted to move forward. Wanted to continue. But, the pain won. So . . . , I let the sword dropt to the ground.

The clatter reminded me how insignificant I was.

The hilt was covered in blood, my blood. I let tears out of my eyes and sobbed, like a weak, pathetic creature. I put my hands on my face covering up the tears.

"So much for a midnight training session." Hax said, standing at the entrance of the courtyard. He leaned on the wall with his hands folded. His grey hair shining in the moonlight.

"Come to gloat?" I say through my teary voice. "No I'm not. I actually came here to help."

"I don't need your help" I spat out. I rubbed my tears away with my palms. "Okay then, I guess you'll have to find someone else to teach you. And the teaching from Father isn't going anywhere by the way."

God, he was right! I mean he is very skillful in battle, and he's my brother so, he wouldn't do this as a joke, and also Fathers teaching just weren't going to cut it. I gathered my voice and erased my tears and said "Fine." . He paused and turned back.

He walked over to me and lay his hand on my shoulder and said "I have an idea".

"Instead of forcefully hitting the target, you hit them with force and sorcery." He explained the concept very clearly and that I would have to embed my sorcery into my blade and strike.

He asked me to stand before the dummy and strike. I looked him in the eyes and I said "I'm already pathetic, I don't want to make myself more pathetic. Maybe this isn't for me."

He rolled his eyes and asked "do you want to prove yourself or not?" I mean . . . I wanted to but, I tried so many times and practiced so many days and nights, I wasn't sure embedding my sorcery into my sword would do anything. But I tried anyway.

I calmed down and collected myself. I took deep breaths and gave my–

"Is this going to take long?" Hax joked while fake yawning. I chuckled and readied to strike. The blade filled with energy and small arcs of my golden lightning was lingering on the sword. I struck the dummy hard.The dummy caught lightning and fell down. It left marks of burnt stuff on it in a lightning pattern.

"Again, but this time harder." Ordered Hax. I

readied the dummy once again and struck. This time I hit harder than before.

It launched its way a few feet on the ground. "Again!" barked Hax. Once again I put everything I had into that strike, My sorcery filled every part of it.

As I watched how the blade swung and the lighting arose, for the first time I felt like I could do this, and I felt a little bit more powerful. So, I let my pain run through me and let it make the blow powerful. Even with feeble magic the blow hit hard. The dummy went flying and hit the brick wall. It snapped into two pieces and fell to the ground. Still having lighting coming out.

"Major improvement Azen." Hax clapped and chuckled. I chuckled too in spite of snort coming out of my nose

CHAPTER 2

After that night of training, a good six years have passed and I became a young man. To this day I am still training, becoming more. I have become more powerful and good in battle.

If my 14 year old self would look at me now, he would be very proud.

My mind trailed off thinking about these thoughts, but the cut which tore open on my arm brought me back to my senses. I looked to the other side of the training hall and Hax was running straight at me. He had his sword open, ready to strike me.

I shook my head and exhaled and waited for him to reach me.

Then I teleported myself "Inuae". I was now behind him. He came to a screeching halt and turned. He threw his blade to me. I barely dogged it, as it caressed my cheek. Then I received a punch in the face and I was swept back.

This was one of our training sessions and injuries are meant to happen. But, we only have to train with weapons.

"Hey! Use your weapons, Idiot". I complain.

"Sorry". Hax said as he snickered. Bet he didn't mean it.

He gave his hand to me. I got up and we started again. We were waiting for someone to make the first move. I studied his expression carefully under the sunlight coming in from the windows of the hall. He brushed his silver hair with his hands. His sword was on the floor.

"Viner". He ordered and the sword flew to his hand. He readied the sword. But, he wasn't moving. We were in a stalemate.

I thought about why I needed to win this round. I

needed the recognition, the self esteem. So that I can finally prove myself. All of those nights spent training flooded my brain. It reminded me how far I've come and how much pain I've endured. So, I can win the Aztheon.

The Aztheon is a hundreds of years old tradition of the three houses, where warriors and fighters participated in a set of five challenges. And in the end one would win. This is a high stakes competition. This was where I could prove myself.

So, to start this match and take what's mine , I said "Volare". His feet were dragging him to me. He tried to ground himself by digging his sword between the floorboards.

"Volare". His feet lifted from the ground and came flying to me. I charged my blade and hit him in the stomach with the flat part of the sword.

He went across the room and slid all the way to the wall. He wheezed out a couple of choughs and groans.

"Good–" He coughed "--Job". "Why thank you" I said as I grinned. I walked over to him and offered him my hand.

"Ready for another round?" I smiled. He took my hand and got up. "Always." He said while letting out another chough.

"Hope your training is going well boys. You do know the Aztheon is coming up in a few days." Father said while standing at the door.

"Yes Father. We were training for it." Hax explained. I had seen my father before but not like this. He seemed a bit happy compared to his normal and usual straight face of a King.

He walked over to me while springing his dark brown hair back. He laid both his hands on my shoulders and said "Good. Good to see you two training together." He also looked over to Hax, laid his hand on his shoulder and spat "Now! Get ready for dinner with the Salem Coven." He glanced at both of us and said "Both of you."

"Alright, alright!" Hax raised his hands and exited the room.

Just as I started to walk, Father called. This was it, this was the moment, maybe now he sees how far I've come, how much progress I made since the weak pastself. He trained me and my brother our whole life to embark on the victory of The Aztheon. To bring home that honor. To prove who was a true Cortian blood.

He looked me in the eyes and said "Son, I need you to be the main person at the dinner. The Coven's deal needs to be secured. Do you understand?"

What!

No *You did great son* or *I'm proud of you son*. No nothing. I worked so hard but nonetheless I'm not recognised. I was angry and disappointed in myself. What more did I need to achieve?

That's it!

I need to win the Aztheon. That would prove I'm worthy.

I kept hope in time. Maybe in time he'll realize.

"Fine." I headed to my room.

It was getting late and the time for dinner was arising. I got ready in the colours of the kingdom. Gold shirt and black trousers.

I heard a knock on the door and a voice said "The dinner's starting, your highness".

I rush to the tower and I climb the endless spiral stairs to reach the grand hall.

It was beautiful this time of night when the sun just set and shades of blue coloured the sky. The Hall had two arches open to the balconies on either side. The pillars lined the walls. Meters of ivy grew on the pillars. A fireplace was situated on the wall to keep the cold of the night away. The curtains blew to the wind and swayed.

People filled the room, holding drinks and talking and socializing. This room was only used a couple of times. And I had seen it when it was empty. But, now with people everywhere it felt more lively.

A general said "His Majesty is there your Highness". He pointed to Father who was discussing with some generals and a group of hooded figures.

They must be the Salem Coven. They are from the House of Covens, a member of Cortis. Their House is one of the best at harnessing the elements of nature. Their House is dated hundreds of centuries ago.

I try to avoid them and head to the delicious snacks table to munch down on some strawberries. God, I was hungry. I hadn't eaten since morning.

After a refreshing drink, I finally head towards Father to greet them.

"Son! I would like you to meet the Salem Coven." He patted me on the back and I greeted them. I could count six of them who had the hoods down and I assume the leader stood before me with his hood down.

He had rings of all sorts, silver, gold, rubies and sapphires. He wore multiple long necklaces made of silver and some made of rope. He had a deathly face. He was paler than the moon. Even though he is still alive. His lips were the lightest shade of pink. He had long black hair and some of the locks were tied.

He looked oddly familiar. I was sure I had read about them in some books.

"Sir Lord Viscount." He offered me his hand.

I knew him, he is the House leader of The Covens. I read legends and myths about him. Before he was a Vampire and roamed the land of Heave. A group of witches turned him into a Wizard while making him immune to the sun. He later killed all of the seven witches in rage and fury.

I returned the shake hand and he smiled. His sharp canines revealed themselves as he smiled.

"Prince Azen Cortis".

"I've heard a lot about you from your father." His voice was raspy and cold. Every word he spoke was as old as him. He was a very old vampire, even older than the House itself.

They had come to the land of souls as pilgrims. To entrust the Aztheon in their hands. This year House of Covens was the host to the games. Every year The games were different, holding different challenges. Only the best of the best survive.

We have some talk and the dinner ends. I was the one to exit so early. I just wanted to retreat to the warmth of my room and stay there alone.

CHAPTER 3

The night was calm and cool. Wind swayed from my window making the curtains swing. I laid on my bed obviously trying to sleep. But, it seems sleep isn't going to come. I stare at the night sky drawing on the roof of my room. A simple art mimicking the real night sky.

All of Sols slept but I remained. I got up and neared the window. The wind blew at me, graciously. I took in the night air. The view from my bedroom is the best. The tower was tall so I could gaze at the entire Sols.

The moon was bright, illuminating the dunes of buildings. Ithink about whether to go or not. It had been a sleepless night and I often did go out on those nights.

Why not now?

I got up the window and crouched on the window frame. I took one last look at Sols, and I dived. I went legs first.

Tardous

I slowed down and landed on the rooftop of a building. I run roof to roof. My soul was refreshed. All those days in the palace I forgot how beautiful it was out here. Because I felt like I belonged here and not inside those walls of the castle.

This was freeing. I had been sneaking out late at night whenever I felt like it. As I jumped from roof to roof I could see the ground beneath and I felt like I was actually flying. I took in every view, every breath. After so many days.

These were my final days of free enjoyment. The Aztheon is going to begin in a few days. Might as well I enjoy these days.

I climbed a church and sat on the roof near the cross. I flayed my legs and thought as I looked at the star covered sky.

I've always wanted to be alone, of course I was always alone in that castle. Hax would be there for some. But, I felt an absence. Like I felt like a part of me was missing. It was my future better self.

Dad was hard and cold hearted. My mother died even before I knew her. Maybe she would have been kind and caring. See me run around and play outside. Make me meals that would melt my heart.

I was trained not to be too attached to human emotions. He wanted me to be like him. A fearless and hard warrior. But he never knew the real me.

Tell me who you are.

A voice called out inside me.

I was compassionate, optimistic. Sure, I would sometimes lose my temper. I am not like my Father, Sometimes I feel like we're both two opposite persons. But me and my brother are best friends having each other's back. Since I had lost so much in my life I feel like I have to be like them. My mother for example.

The nights when I fled, I often caught some thieves. I thought about it because I heard the church doors opening. It was later than midnight. Why would church officials be here, at this time?

I looked down, to see the door closed. I drop down to investigate more deeply. The gates were open slightly. The lock was broken and on the ground in pieces.

Thieves.

Definitely. I slid through the gap and entered the church. It was pitch black. I couldn't see anything. Only I could hear some footsteps. I carefully observed and heard.

As my eyes adjusted to the dark, I could see a silhouettes against the moonlight coming in from the high windows of the church. The two were scurrying to get something from the altar.

"Stop! Freeze!". As soon as I say the words The person runs.

Lux.

Light filled the church as a small fireball floated. I could see now. The person was a She. she wore a mask, so I was unable to see her face clearly. She climbed to the windows and left.

She saw me as she w as heading out. I could see from the upper revealed portion of her face that she had a scar on her eyebrow and had dark hair.

I rushed to catch the dark haired thief. I ran out and followed the thief. She was on the roof trying to escape. She held the stolen goods in a cloth held tightly in her arms. I was running faster and faster. And she did too. She tripped on a tile and fell rolling down. She wheezed a chough. I halted before her. She got up and stood her ground.

"Are you hurt? Do you need help?" I said. She was a thief and they didn't care about our help.

She spat out "I don't need your help". As Soon as she finished saying that, She sent a sharp flower stalk at me. I dodged it. It fell on the ground and the ground turned black. It eroded the stone pavement, and sharp thorns punctured the stone.

If that would have hit me, I would have been very dead. She was a witch nonetheless, utilizing the elements and using cursed weapons.

As I turned back to face her, she was gone. Never once had someone escape me. Either I would have let them go on purpose or I would have caught them.

Ugh.

I had accepted my defeat as I ran my finger through my hair. She was obviously a good fighter and a master at sneaking around. It's very rare to find talented and skillful people in

Sols, especially in combat. Nice to see similar people in life who get it. For now I only have Hax as my buddy.

Little drops patted on my shoulder. Slowly beginning as a drizzle and working its way up to a shower. Dark clouds loomed over and blocked the moon. I turned and ran to the castle.

I got to the castle's gates , I climbed them and jumped over. It got to the foot of my tower. By now the rain was heavy and wetted me from top to bottom.

I put my hold on the first brick which was slippery and made it a few feet up without crashing. I carefully put my hand on the sturdy spots and worked my way up. I was almost there, I looked to Sols and took in the view, because this would be my last look at this place. The rain made it so that I could see only upto a distance. But, the random flashes of lightning illuminated the city.

I reached my room and climbed inside. I was gasping for air and clearing my eyes from water. Water soaked me thoroughly and dripped down to make a puddle of water.

CHAPTER 4

Light poked my eyes and the warmth of it fell on my face. It was morning. The soft chirps of birds and water droplets falling from the window sill indicated that the rain had stopped.

I struggled to get out of bed as I lay in my sheets. I opened my eyes and welcomed the morning sunlight. I stretched and yawned. Quickly overthrowing the sheets I look outside. The daybreak filled the city in light.

As I looked down I saw banters of The House of Covens and coloured in Purple. There were also banters of The House of Death and life in their respective black and green colours. People from all of the houses entered the castle.

What's today? Why such a grand entrance?

I recollect my thoughts. And wonder. Something was gonna happen.

What is it?

They aren't here for dinner, because that happened yesterday. Someone could have died. No, no one is too old or famous that I know of.

Crap!

It's the Aztheon. Of course I forgot the most important event in my life. I quickly throw on my clothes and head out to the hall. I looked and I heard chatter coming from beneath.

They were in the Dining hall. I ran down to the doors of the hall. They were open. Inside, a bunch of people from different houses talked and chatted. The tables were set aside to the wall. Amidst the crowd I could see Lord Viscount gathering on the pedestal.

I rush inside to not miss anything important. I slid

between people to reach the front.

"A little late, aren't you?" Hax whispered beside me. I asked "What happened? No one said anything to me about anything."

"Me too. They barged in this morning." The Aztheon wasn't supposed to be for another few days.

Lord Viscount brought attention "Ahm. Good Morning fellow people and Aztheon contestants. I came here to receive the contestants for the Aztheon, some of you may wonder why it has come early. The reason why it has come so early is due to some classified reasons that I cannot explain."

Cannot explain? Why not? I mean conducting the competition unexpectedly has never happened in the history of it. There must be some reasons that he can explain.

"Nevertheless, Let us not ruin the spirit of this sacred competition, gifted to us by our ancestors. An age-old tradition happening every century." He paused, catching his breath. "Let us continue with our enrollment of contestants."

He called upon the people who wanted to participate to come forward. Hax and I stepped up along with some other people.

I observed the faces of the people there. From sols only 8 members I could count from far away took part.

The lord Took the contestant's hands and cut deep into the palm of their hands. He collected them in a goblet. After another they enrolled, now it was Hax's turn. The Lord took his hand with great strength and cut. He winced in pain. He went down and sucked the blood.

That was painful no doubt. But, less than the pain I will experience in the Aztheon. I could turn back now. Retreat and not risk my life.

No.

I won't turn back. Not now, when I had come all this way. I bravely gave my right hand. Without thinking he cut a slit without my notice.

I sucked my teeth and bore the pain. I got down to the crowd and waited for the others to enroll.

While I was looking around I saw a familiar person. I only saw her dark brown hair. Or maybe it was a guy with really long hair. No, they were She, looking from the body language and posture.

Not thinking too much, I looked around again. I saw a guy who stood after me in the line for the enrollment. He had short blonde hair and wore a white poncho. Preferably a Life reader. I also saw a woman In an extravagant black poncho with stitchings made with silk. She wore a ponytail of dark hair.

She seemed to be royalty. I had guessed as she returned to her parents who were also dressed beautifully.

I also saw some witches, in a group of three. A separate coven.

The Lord said, regaining the attention of the crowd "The

Aztheon will take place in Heave. The contestants will be gathered together and will be transported to Heave tonight. For now, get your rest and enjoy this day, because the Aztheon will begin tomorrow."

The crowd broke into cheers and goblets of wine were being cheered and drunk.

~X~

I gathered my weapons, clothes and other extra stuff and packed–, technically shoved them into my suitcase. It was almost midnight now. The lanterns of my room burned bright as it cast an orange glow.

As I finished packing, I looked at my blade. It had markings etched into it. They were the burnt metal formed by the lightning. I rubbed my thumb on it. I remembered my brother and my father and how far I've come. The feeling of excitement and fear shivered through my spine. The feeling of winning and losing. No matter what my decision is already locked in as I gave my blood to the Lord.

After the grand party, I felt tired. After also eating too many slices of apple pie, I grew weary. So, I slept. Just a nap, I would wake up before the trip.

~X~

I opened my eyes as I felt more refreshed. I felt like I was in a field of grass. I felt so calm and centered. Then I heard a scream, then another. I rushed to see what was going on. I was in a forest, blue lights were scattered around and I found my sword laying on the ground. Then I heard another scream and a wild beast's snarl.

The Aztheon had started.

CHAPTER 5

The screams continued. I was all alone only with my blade and blue balls of lights on the forest ground. The trees loomed over, and laid on top of each other. No light ray enters through the trees. It was like we were locked in.

I climbed a tree to see outside. I couldn't tell if it was night or day. I got a higher branch and tried to climb to the top. The leaves and branches acted like a ceiling Not a hard or rigid one, but a never ending hedge of leaves. I drop down to explore the dark forest.

Mist rolled in from all sides. It was only up to the knee level. The humidity made me sweat. I started walking through the dense grass with my blade in my hand. I began to recognise the place. It was an enchanted forest having powers only possessed at night. Assuming it was the same time when we left. According to all the conditions it would be the Widow forest, in Heave.

The screamings calmed down and the snarls reduced. I was still walking in the lit up areas and being very attentive.

The blade hilt was covered in my sweat, and my whole body was wet. Wet locks of hair clung to my head that covered my eyes.

I scanned the environment and saw nothing. Nothing but endless darkness just a few feet away.

What were we supposed to do. What was the end or goal of this round. This swirl of confusion spinned my stomach making me go nauseous or maybe it was the humidity of the darkness which made me feel like that.

I hear a howl near me. I ready my position to the sound. Then leaves crumbled somewhere in the distance. I was looking here and there. Then I saw a pair of red eyes in the darkness, maybe a few feet above the ground.

Slowly the monster came out of the darkness. Its fur was rugged and ruffled. Its teeth were humongous. The whole size of it reached the trees. It was a Howl, a giant rabid dog.

My feet trembled but I gained stability. The Howl was growling, red eyes set on me. If I wanted to escape I couldn't go anywhere but back. The blue lights cast an eerie glow on it.

We were waiting to make a move. I needed some distance between me and the Howl at all times. So, I ran. It followed. I created some distance between it.

"Imperium".

I threw my blade through the trees and it hit. It created a massive cut on its side and silver bubbles came out.They were sort of liquid but at the same time not. The silver insides spewed out and the liquid disappeared. It slowled and decreased in size.

I stopped and observed. The monster jumped for me. It landed on me, making me pinned to the ground. It was heavy making me unable to move. Its head reached me. I threw my arms around the neck and stopped it from reaching me.

Maybe It was time to accept my defeat. My arms grew tired and The dog growled even more. Its claws scratched my left side of the torso. I screamed loudly. Panicking, I started to think. Anything which could help me.

My blade.

"Volare".

The blade came flying at blazing speeds. It punctured the skull of the creature and a plethora of fluids and silver insides fell on my face.

I throw the dog to the side. I got up and wiped my face so that I could see clearly. The monster got smaller and smaller. At last it became a deflated skin suit.

~X~

I walked and walked, miles on end. The end of the forest was nowhere in sight. Endless canopy of the trees and endless darkness. I was tired and my legs began to give out. My blade felt heavier and heavier, with each step. I barely could hold my head straight. My eyes felt like weights were attached to it.

Locks of hair clung to my forehead, dripping sweat on my face. I stopped and didn't continue to walk. I plopped right there on the ground. My vision was blurry.

No, I had to stay awake. The forest has predators.

I tried to get up, but my limbs aren't responding. I didn't sleep for the last endless grueling hours. My fight with the Howl made it even worse. My eyes closed. But I struggled and opened them.

CHAPTER 6

The wind breezes, and pink leaves fall on my face gently. The sunlight woke me, all the while being gentle. The trees' canopy was reduced, letting in light. The forest no longer trapped me.

Hax's face loomed over me. "Ah finally awake!"

I raise my head and say "What?" Hax rolls his eyes "You fell asleep and I had to carry you all the way here" He paused "So, you're welcome".

"From where?" I look around. Contestes are gathered and chatter in the forest. The forest was now calm during the day. Beautiful pink trees surround us.

"If I hadn't carried you all the way here you would have been one of them." Hax pointed to a pile of dead bodies. Ones that had failed to survive the first trial. Ones that didn't belong.

I got up as Hax offered me a hand. I sweep away the leaves on me. And looked at the survivors. There were eighteen in total left, including me and Hax. Who were from the initial twenty five. Everyone had cuts and bruises and were badly injured. I got a sharp pain from my side and remembered I too had a deep cut.

"Nasty cut, right?" Hax said. I lift up my shirt to see a black scar formed on the wound.

I ignored the cut as it would only make me look weak. My vision wandered back to the crowd. From which I recognised some of them. Like the blonde life reader and the death reader girl.

The crowd was standing near a tall gate at the end of the forest. The gate opened silencing the crowd.

The Salem coven walked in along with Lord Viscount. "Congratulations Contestants! You're one of the few to survive the first round, unlike . . ." He pointed at the unlucky contestants who lay lifeless on the ground, blood dripping to form a puddle.

"Anyway vamonos to the preparation for the next trial! The wonderful city of Heave awaits you" The crowd followed him outside the gate to the lifeless savannah. He guided us to the cart waiting for us.

Some of us went in the first one and Hax and others in another. Out of the people there, the blonde life reader who was sitting across from me said "Pretty nasty scar there" He sucked his teeth "I'm Eliot"

He offered me his hand. But I didn't take it

"I've gotten worse." I simply say. The cart rattled on the rough ground as we spoke

"I can heal it for you" He offered.

Does he think I'm weak?

I simply give him no answer. "Ok, don't trust people. I get it".

The death reader girl who sat next to him said "Stop Eliot, we shouldn't talk to our opponents, let alone offer them help."

The conversion ended there as the girl scoffed while adjusting her black outfit. "But Bea." Elliot said. The girl, supposedly Bea, shot a look at him and he shut up. They seemed to be siblings.

We rode the rest of the way in awkward silence and while shooting glares at each other.

~X~

The walls were tall and made of stone. I could see buildings and roofs over the walls. The large wooden gates opened revealing the beautiful city hiding inside.

Beautiful two story buildings made of bricks form the ground and have wide view windows into the upperstories. The glare and reflected on the windows casting wonderful lighting all over the place.

There was a palace in the distance up on a gentle hill. The architecture was glorious, mimicking the bricked glass wall of the city.

We were on the path to the palace to stay with the royalty of Jade.

~X~

We reached the bridge to the humongous palace. Bigger than the one in Sols dare I say. A gradient of red brick fading away as it goes to the top. The glass of all different colours covered the dome and the pointy roof at the end. As the sun was setting its light reflected on the palace like strings of light attached to it and had colourful shadows of the glass. At the top it had a wonderful piece of red jade, the specialty of this place.

Once again the gates opened to the road that circled the palace. The cart stopped as we came close to the building. We all dropped from the cart to gather at the majestic piece of art awaiting before us.

"Beautiful isn't it." Elliot snapped while looking at the building with glowing eyes.

"First time? Me too." I gave him a reply.

"If the *staring in awe* is over, let's actually get inside." Hax slipped through between us getting to the Lord who was already at the palace gates.

"Follow me people or you'll get lost in this maze." The lord ordered while following through the gates.

The eighteen of us followed him into the building. There was a dome which was made of glass. The evening sun made an array of colors . Pillars surrounded the circular room. In the middle was a tree like the one we had seen in the Widow forest. Beautiful and elegant in its pink glory.

There she stood. The queen of Jade, Fiona. In her outstanding beauty. She wore a bun of red hair and a red jade coloured dress having grey smoke come out the bottom. Like the architecture of the palace, her dress was covered in broken shards of colourful glass. She had extensive red makeup on her face and wore many red jade jewels. If there was anything more red than this I would be surprised.

The crowds' murmurs dropped as the queen opened her mouth to speak "Evening contestants! Once again I'm so glad to see you."

Once again?

The crowd again broke into murmur "Yes, I've been watching all since the Aztheon had started." She quickly gave an answer.

"Of course she would. She's the queen for god's sake!" Hax whispered in my ear. "She is probably listening to us right now." I say.

She turned to us with a bland face and said "Yes I am, Cortian brothers."

We hurry to attentive positions and listen the rest of the way. "The next trial will be held in a few days. As for this evening, you can change and attend the Welcome dinner."

CHAPTER 7

The red coloured shirts and pants of all different colours were hanging in front of me. Each shirt wasn't identical, some were in different textures and some had different shades of red. There were also suits and ties.

I choose a red shirt to wear over my black trousers and cover with a black vest and a gold tie, all neatly styled.

The light came in from the wide floor to ceiling windows. The sun was setting as it painted pink shades of the sky. The room was medium sized.

A bed was stationed in front of the window, between. The floor was marble and had been polished to perfection. The bed was red and had a white rug beneath. The ceiling was stone, uncut and rugged.

I say goodbye to my room and continue to head to the main hall. It was tall and circular. The other half of the hall had tall colourful glass. Lights lit up the dark night. People were already there all in red drenched outfits. Marbled floors and tall pillars hugged the walls. Music played on the pianos and harps.

Circular tables were set and food was served. I spotted Hax

wearing a red tuxedo with his mop of silver hair. I also saw Elliot and Bea talking to the Queen.

I took a glass of red wine and headed to the crowd of people. I see Hax talking to someone while drinking. I tried to see clearly what was going on.

He was talking to a girl who had worn a red cloak which covered her head.

"Meet Drianna. Another fellow contestant. She's a witch" Hax explained. She took off her hood and revealed a girl with dark brown hair and an elegant face. She also had a scar on her eyebrow.

The thief!

It was her. The one I had chased that night. The witch who had deadly flowers for weapons. And a scar on her eyebrow

"You." I growled at her., for almost killing me with a flower.

She also growled "You, again"

Hax's face was in an expression for confusion. He asked, bewildered, "You two know each other?"

"You participated in the Aztheon? I haven't seen you since" I asked because I hadn't seen her since that night.

"Of course you didn't, because your legs were so weak you couldn't even catch me."

What does that have to do with me not seeing her?

Maybe she had been there, because I saw a familiar dark haired girl.

"Wait a minute, what does that have to do with him not being able to you?" Hax intervened watching us fight like it was some drama.

Exactly!

"At Least I didn't fall off the roof, Denise." I said. She gasped and Hax snickered and laughed.

"My name is Drianna!" She shot off into the crowd and disappeared.

"I know!" I said to her as she disappeared.

"Hey, maybe you shouldn't be so mean."

I gave him a guilty look, then Hax and I found a table to sit by the whole evening. People danced, ate and socialized

I hate parties.

Socializing and everything in general. It was like venturing into the jungle filled with challenges and you were blindfolded.

You never knew what would happen next. One

moment someone comments about your outfit and in the other you do something embarrassing.

That's why I like to be alone. No one else to satisfy than yourself. This was all common since I only had Hax as my brother and friend.

This was also why I went early to my bedroom at the other dinner in Sols.

God I miss Sols.

I really did. The familiar environment was much more comfortable than this unknown place and this glass building.

It was around midnight when I finished a couple glasses of the wine and went to get some more. I stood at the counter waiting for the guy to pour me a drink. I looked over to the door from which I had entered the hall.

The same girl with the red cloak on was heading out. In a sort of hurried way. I don't know if it was the wine or something else but, I followed her.

She took turns in the corridors like she knew it like the back of her hand. I followed at a distance from her. So that she wouldn't notice and that I would keep an eye on her.

She drew near the exit. She took out keys from her pockets

and proceeded to open the doors. She opened them slightly, only letting her fit through the gap.

I had been hiding in the turn where she last took and peeked to see. As the door began to close, I sprinted to get through the tiny gap.

I barely managed to fit through the gap. Then I entered the dark night. It was hard to see. I put my body close to the door and let my eyes adjust.

The small stars in the sky became visible and I could see Drianna walking over the bridge. I followed and kept my distance. Slowing down and speeding up to keep the same distance from us at all times.

She didn't turn anywhere this time and headed down the straight road which led to the gates. Her cloak was very visible in bright red as she whooshed to the gate.

When we reached the gate, I could make out someone who was on the other side of the gate. They were sitting on a horse. I couldn't see what he looked like as the night was too dim.

She reached into her pocket and proceeded to give a letter to the person. They toolkit and turned their horse around and retreated into the savannah.

I went near her and tapped her shoulder. She turned around swiftly and gasped in fright.

"What are you doing here?" She asks.

She was obviously suspicious and acting strange like I was the one who had swept off into the night and continued to submit a mysterious letter.

"I could ask the same." I simply question her.

Her face turned to an emotion which resembled that she had done something secret.

"It was–" she shook her head "Nothing."

She is hiding something, even more obviously. She quickly wore her hood and tried to hide her face. Her hands were behind her back and she fidgeted.

"What did you deliver?" I questioned about the thing she gave to the person on the horse.

Maybe a letter to loved ones, or something even more secret.

She put on a forced confessed look "What horse?"

"The one that was outside the gates." I pressed on.

"A letter." she said, "To whom?" I asked immediately.

Her face turned into disgust "Why do you care?'"

She also murmured something that I couldn't totally hear but could make out that it sounded like – *You didn't care before.*

She was hiding something and I will find out what.

She muttered "You won't be here when you find out." she gave an evil smirk and plunged a small needle into my stomach.

I could say what happened but what happened, happened fast.

First I felt light headed and then my vision started to spin. Before I could figure out what was going out, colours of all sorts filled my vision and then I had closed my eyes. Plunging me into darkness.

CHAPTER 8

The grey haired man walked to the woman. At the party the two stood at the gate.

The grey haired man spoke "Got it done? The firefly?"

The woman leaned closer. "An interruption occurred, but The firefly was delivered."

The man thought and rolled his eyes, signalling his annoyance to the woman.

"Him?" The man asked, sipping his wine. The woman nodded

"You have to hide it from him." The woman whispered to his ear. "He can't know."

"Working on it." another sip.

The woman now folded her hands and said "You've kept it from that father of yours. Struggling to keep it from that brother."

The man's face now turned sour. He pointed his finger to her and said "Don't call him that, he's not my father. And maybe he's not my brother but he's my friend."

The woman stood down and said, "You're gonna have to kill him eventually, right? I'm just making sure you know that."

The man rubbed the wine glass with his thumb and was lost in thought. "Yeah. . . . eventually."

He seemed to have mercy for his friend. But not enough to

suppress the group. Not enough that he would falter his own plans. Not enough to reveal his lifetime act.

He took another sip. "Where is he?" The man asked

"In his room." The woman took the glass of wine from him and took a sip. "Asleep."

"You didn't kill him right?" The man's concern grew.

"No, just gave him a small dose. He's sound asleep." The woman took a sip before handing it back to the man.

The Woman put on her hood and said "It's late, I'm already sleepy. And wine is the last thing I need." She walked off and exited the party.

The man was still here sipping on wine and thinking. Thinking about when he would kill.

He knew he was acting, but they had become closer as friends, as. . . . brothers.

He wiped that thought from his mind. He knew neither were his family. Nothing could stop him from achieving his revenge.

But, could his friend? Could his brother?

CHAPTER 9

I woke up in my room with fuzzy memories of that night. My face was really tired, and I was hungover. I could barely open my eyes. I had woken up in my room. Golden morning sunlight came in through the windows behind me.

I threw the sheets over and started to get dressed. That night, She gave something to someone. She still hadn't answered my question. I thought as I buttoned my white shirt, and threw on a red jacket.

I go out through the door to grab some breakfast down at

the dining hall. The doors were open to a hall no one other than the contestants were present. The gigantic hall felt empty with only eighteen here for breakfast.

I immediately spotted some blueberry muffins on one of the tables that were to the far left of the rectangular hall. Without care I chugged them into my mouth.

Eating food after a hangover is so good.

As I started to grab more food, Hax bumped me on my back and came standing beside me.

"Still hungover?" Hax tilted his head as he asked. He too

put food on a plate like a human, while I was eating like a wild animal.

"Yaugh." I said as the food was muffling my words, I gulped and repeated "Yeah."

I put on a confused look. How could Hax know about this? I thought that Drianna brought me to my room.

"Wait, how do you-" Hax interrupted me. "Yeah, Drianna told me all about you. You suspected that she was doing something illegal" He paused "And that you accused her, but you let her go."

Hax burst out into laughter. "What's so funny about that?" I said, being obviously embarrassed .

"No, no. It's just that you literally were acting like sworn enemies during the party, and now you're acting like friends." He barely managed to get those words out of his mouth while laughing.

"And one more thing, the next trial requires a team." He explained as his laughter calmed down.

'When did they tell–. Okay I'm not going to even ask and probably answer the question myself. The queen told you when I was out following her."

"Exactly. And guess who our team mate is besides you

and me." Hax raised his eyebrow and tilted his head towards me.

No. Not her.

"Drianna?" He nodded his head. I . . . have no words. This wasn't going to work out, we hate each other. When are we supposed to train? The next trial could be in days. We both need to cooperate and work together. That wouldn't be possible after yesterday's encounter. She would hate me.

"Training starts today on the grounds. Pack your things."

-X-

The training grounds were behind the majestic palace. The grounds had no walls or borders. The sky was clear with only a few clouds.

There were exactly four grounds ,three of them already full. Hax and I gathered together on the last ground and ready ourselves while we waited for the other.

It was almost a half an hour after we arrived, and Drianna finally appeared on the ground.

"Where were you? Come on, we have to train." Hax readied his position.

But, Drianna interrupted, "I'm not training."

I put on a puzzled look on my face. She was still in her red cloak.

"Why?" I asked. "Got some work to do." She quickly replied.

What work? She was just invited to our team and doesn't even contribute.

I can't blame her though.

"It's okay. We'll train without you." I paused. "We'll catch up later."

Hax, signaled something to her. Probably a wave of goodbye, and she retreated into the palace.

I turned to face Hax on the grounds. The afternoon sun

was casting a shadow on Hax's face.

He ran his fingers through his grey hair and readied his position again.

My scar on my torso was healing just enough so that I could move easily.

I too readied my position with my sword.

"Only sparing Azen." Hax set the rules.

I smirk "Don't want to get kicked by your younger brother, do you?" I tighten the grip.

He shook his head and said "Fine, but I won't be responsible if you get hurt before the trial."

Challenge on.

I hold the sword in my right and run toward Hax. I strike him, but he blocks retracting me a bit back. I take one more strike. This time his parry did not match.

Between the clinking and clanking of the blades, I took one strike to the stomach. Luckily the leather armour stopped the cut.

Hax and I striked at the same time, resulting in a moment of stand off.

"This is counter intuitive. We are supposed to fight together, not fight against each other." Hax said at the moment.

I'm still holding the standoff saying "Oh yeah." I pause to blow my hair from my view. "Already losing?" Hax chuckles and retreats giving distance between.

My fingers tightened and adrenaline rushed through my body.

The sun moved through the sky as we trained after we fought. The afternoon turned into the evening. And with the evening the sun set, bringing upon the night.

At night, people slept until morning.

But . . . The trial began.

CHAPTER 10

The waves washed ashore. Bringing water to wet me. With every wave I became aware of where I was. Slowly with each calm crash of the wave. I opened my eyes.

My face was on the sand which half of my face was covered with. I was washed astray on the beach. The tropical sun glared upon me, drying me of the water.

I got up, wiggled the sand and wiped my face to remove the chunky sand stuck to it.

As I did get up I observed that the forest was creeping onto the beach line.

This definitely was not the Widows, as this forest had green leafed trees while it had pink ones. Also considering the beach as Jade was far from any sea.

This place didn't even look remotely close to any of the kingdoms.

Then I felt something in my pocket. I reached inside to recover a piece of paper, which had a message written in black ink, which was now leaking into the paper because of the water. It read.

BEHOLD THE SECOND TRIAL. THE CONTESTANTS MUST REACH THE TOP OF THE TREE WITH THEIR TEAM WHILST SURVIVING THE IMPENDING DANGER THAT LURK IN THE WOODS.

WHO EVER MAKES IT TO THE TOP BEFORE SUN DOWN WILL BE PROMOTED TO PARTICIPATE IN THE LAST AND FINAL TRIAL OF THE AZTHEON.

GOOD LUCK TO ALL THE CONTESTANTS AND HOPE THEY MAKE IT

I looked at the giant tree in the center of the forest, overshadowing the canopy of the forest. It had branches stemming out towards the sky and an immense cover of leaves cast a shadow.

That was where I needed to get to with my teammates. Get to the top before sundown and while surviving the monsters.

The tree was anywhere from five to seven kilometers inside the forest. By the position of the sun, it is likely to be well past afternoon. Which meant I had to reach fast.

The first lurked and called me to go in and finish this trial.

Because after this the last trial would be held.

Just one more to the finale.

I thought about winning the Aztheon and pictured myself. But none of it was going to become true unless I moved.

I came back to my senses and found myself still at the edge of the forest. I moved towards the forest. When I reached the edge I heard all sorts of noises, some of which were birds and animals, but I heard some unnatural sounds echoing through the dense trees.

Silencing my fears I took a stride into the forest.

With every step the forest covered most of my view. A few feet into the forest I was engulfed by tall and short trees and grass and dense air.

The smell of the forest was amazing, giving a fruity and fresh aroma. Small rays of light managed to enter through the canopy, lighting the forest.

I was much more than fifty feet into, when leaves rustled in the distance. The small sounds grew into footsteps and the footsteps grew into panting breaths.

Someone was hunting me, or so I thought. Then someone collided with me.

It was Drianne. She shouted "Run!" I was frozen, unable to understand the threat.

"Run! What are you looking at!" She shouted one last time. And I listened.

We both ran ignoring the trees , leaves and twigs hit us as we tried to evade something.

Then Drianne pulled me into the sunlight which was peering through the canopies of the trees, and we stood there. Awaiting the monster.

"What are you doing, I thought we were supposed to run!"

She signaled a loud *Shh!* And pointed to the distance.

I looked closer and heard twigs snapping and leaves rustling. Someone was there out in the distance.

It was *someone* I was sure, the light footsteps and light breathing made it so. Not a monster but someone.

Then he appeared, A tall slender man. He wore a dirty and ragged cloak which had spots of blood over the purple cloak. His face was pale and gray, like all of his blood was squeezed from his body.

Though he looked like a man he was behaving like a wild animal. Snarling and growling as he saw us.

He approached us but we didn't move. Drianne firmly held my hand and we both stood there.

As we stood in the light, the man dared not to come any closer, because when he reached his hand for us it burned. He held his hand in pain.

Then I saw it, he had fangs protruding out of his mouth.

He was a vampire. I knew it as he hesitated to come out into the light and how his skin burned at the touch of it.

After examining a way to escape from the vampire, by consecutively moving between spots of light coming from above the canopy.

Drianne and I ran to each spot and made our way through the forest progressively. .

There was me and Drianne but one was left, One who was also part of this team.

So, I ask "Where is Hax?"

She replied while we were walking through a long spot where the light was the most "Don't know."

I look back to keep an eye out for the vampire and guess. "Maybe he's on the other side."

As I turned my head back she said "Maybe, But not right

now. We need to focus on getting to the tree."

She's right.

She was right, all that matters is how we get to the top. Hax knows how to survive. He'll figure something out. It's not like we can help him from out here

"Do you think he also washed up on a beach?" I asked as I shook off some sand in my hair.

She lifted her shoulders signaling a *'don't know'*

I yawned as we walked, and from time to time looked at the position of the sun to predict the time we had left before sundown. Since we started well past afternoon, I'd say we had a whole three to four hours to reach the tree.

As we walked for another fifteen minutes or so, we heard blasts of magic coming in from the left.

Then two people emerged from the trees who had dragged a dead vampire with them.

CHAPTER 11

The vampire was very dead. Its pale skin was pure white. It looked as though it was made of stone. As I moved my eyes up and down, I saw sprouts of leaves and thorns poking out of it. The thorns and leaves made out of the mouth too.

With the vampire two people also emerged. They were the people responsible for the ugly death of it. They were the exact same people I met at the carriage on our way to Heave.

They were Elliot and Bea. The two of them had made it this far. And doing it so violently. The thorns and leaves were definitely Elliots magic. While on the other hand I am pretty sure that Bea sucked the life out from the vampire before anything.

"Hey!" I yelled. Drianne quickly whispered "You know them?"

Then Elliot waved back at me. He was still in complete contrast to his sister. They both looked tired. Elliot's white robes had stains of dirt, and Bea's had blood stains. The blood was hard to make out from her black robes.

Elliot began to walk towards us and Bea too.

We could all walk towards the tree, considering we don't kill each other. We possibly could. I can, It was all up to Drianne.

"No!" She shouted silently. We were discussing the matter away from them. "Are you stupid? They'll kill us when they get the chance."

I huddled closer and said "This trial doesn't need killing."

She gave me a look of both confusion and annoyance. "When have I ever said something wrong?"

She left and headed to the two. She said to them "We'll work together."

Bea turned over and walked signaling us to follow.

-X-

We walked for another while. While also avoiding the vampires. Now it was starting to get dark. We were almost there. I could see the tree's trunk just off into the distance between the trees.

We were about to finally make it. I could see that the sun was setting too.

Just in time.

I couldn't see anyone here either. Seemed like we were the first ones there. All this time had passed while walking to the tree. All this time there was no Hax. We didn't reach him and he didn't reach us.

Hopefully he's near. Somewhere around here.

The siblings were in front of us. They were leading the way. We walked calmly until here, untill.

"Ah!" Elliot let out a short shriek. He violently shook his legs to get something off.

"What now?" Bea gave an annoyed grunt.

The focus shifted towards Elliot's leg. Something had

grabbed onto him. It was difficult to see. I could make out a long root was hidden under the leaves, which had his leg.

Elliot grunted and tried a few times to get free of it. At Last he had enough. He bent down to remove it.

As he bent down, the root pulled him, making him fall to the ground. The root dragged him.

I quickly rushed to grab him. "Don't let go! Definitely don't let go!" Elliot cried.

Bea raised her arm and the root withered away. "See nothing to be afraid of." she said, unknowing that a root was dangling behind her.

"Bea don't move." Drianne warned. Bea didn't listen and turned. The root grabbed her by the arm and lifted her up into the canopy.

Elliot was on the edge of passing out seeing her sister be grabbed by the plant.

I went to the spot where she stood and looked up and called to her. "Bea!"

Then we heard a shot of magic, and she came plopping down.

Elliot shouted "More!" We all looked to see many roots surrounded us and dangled from the trees. We all gathered as a bunch in the middle, our backs faced each other.

"Elliot, use your life magic to tell them to lay off!" There was a tone of worry in Drianne's voice.

Now Elliot was definitely going to pass out. He got a hold of himself and uttered "Uh . . . really can't do that!"

We had to make it in time. In time for the sunset. If we didn't we would be vulnerable to the vampires. If we were too busy with this problem, we would fail.

To get there fast we would have to avoid the roots and avoid fighting them.

"Run!" I quickly say. Elliot took off first avoiding the waves of the roots. Then it was Bea and Drianne. I was left, standing there helpless.

I too made a jump barely avoiding a slap to the face by one of the roots.

When I got there the others were on the climb to the top. Drianne and I started last and hurried to get a foothold on the tree.

Once we did we climbed *fast.* "Quickly!" I said to her,

We climbed to a big branch high off the ground. I helped Drianne up, "Whew!" She calmed herself steadying her breath.

Just then she was swept off her feet. A root dragged her. With my reflexes I grabbed her.

It all happened in slow motion. The root grabbing her, and me taking her hand, and me seeing her face change into sad and helpless.

There were no tears in her eyes but the sunlight made it so that I observed tear drops in her eyes.

In that moment I chose *not* to *let go*.

I saw that same dark brown haired girl with a scar for an eyebrow nearly die in front of me. The same girl who I had insulted.

"Hold On!!" I cried. She shook her head telling me she'll hold on. I pulled with all my strength.

I buckled but didn't let go of her. I held on tightly and pulled her up.

I stuck her ankle which had the root. It whimpered and died. Letting her free.

She looked at me with immense gratitude, for saving her life. But she didn't know it was for all that I said to her.

Somehow I made it right.

CHAPTER 12

The sky was bright orange. The sun was almost setting. We were stationed on top of the tree. We relaxed on the huge bed of leaves. There was no sign of Hax, even now. If he won't make it before sunset he'll be eliminated.

"You think he'll make it here?" Drianne asked worriedly. I turned my head from the sunset. I saw her face.

It was good to see her face, since she . . . Now I had noticed her, more than ever. We became friends.

"He will." I said to her, "You know him right."

Now to think of it, how does she know him? On that night Has just revealed that he had a friend. And . . . on the same night she snuck out, secretly.

I picked up the courage to ask her. "How do you know Hax?"

She stuttered, and did not say anything for a second. She looked at the sunset and turned back.

"Business." she tilted her head and laughed it off, not drawing attention.

What kind of business?

I meant to ask. But, I didn't want to trouble her. So I kept my mouth shut and continued to watch the sunset with her.

The sun was nearly over the horizon. It was orange. It was setting upon the water. Its reflections moved on the water. The air caused distortions on the sun.

Peace.

I felt at peace for the first time in the Aztheon. Not having to care for anything but to sit and relax.

We heard rustling in the leaves below us. We looked back to see Elliot and bea sitting there silently.

It wasn't them.

Slowly someone came out of the leaves emerging in the dying light of the sun.

He stood up revealing himself to us. As the sun set the darkness came up his neck to his chin. At that he smiled. The darkness moved up his face and fully covered him.

Hax.

"Hax!" Shouted Drianne.

It was the person I loved most, my brother. The same person who grew up with me, who had immense power, being a part of the Cortian kingdom, The same one with a whole lot of mysteries hidden with him, the mystery of his connection with Drianne, and her connection to the letter.

This man who had all of this was standing before me. I thought I knew him, no. Now I see. I see his mysteries.

CHAPTER 13

The boots clanged. As the man came down the steps. The metal of his cane hit the rock floor hard, creating an ominous sound.

With each step the sounds grew. At last he entered the dungeon.

He wore a black trousers, black coat, a black scarf and a black hat. He was accompanied by a cane which had a metal skull at the top.

He clutched the cane and learnt against it. The man was of upright posture and was lean as well as tall.

His face wasn't visible. The grey fire of the dungeon lights didn't illuminate enough to show his face.

But with each step, each limp, his face came into view.

Clang.

The man had shrinked skin.

Clang.

The skin was smooth on one end and had burn marks on the other side.

Clang.

He had one eye which was visible.

Clang.

He came to one final stop and leaned his face.

Then it was a full picture. The man was burnt, not completely. His other eye was plucked out, and had gotten a fake eye. It was black devoid of colour except for the pupil which was grey.

"Have we got it?" The man asked. His voice was creaky and sharp. Each word he said had his intentions.

The soldier was stationed opposite to the table. He had a letter in his hand which he had passed to the man.

"Yes Trickster we have got the firefly." The soldier answered, in code.

This man was the Trickster, maybe associated with the Tricks.

He pulled out a small knife from his pocket and used it to tear the sigil on the letter apart.

He opened it and read.

Trickster,
From Fire.
Take this as a sign.
The condition here is normal at best. No one batted an eye, not even Cortis. Don't light the fire. Wait for the oil. Fire will signal Trickster when the oil is poured. Trickster please cooperate. Madam and Fire are pouring the oil. The time to spark will come. Wait.
Let The Fire Burn.

It was all written code, only understandable to him.

His face got red and he crumpled the letter in his hand. He pounded his hand on the table.

"Don't light the Fire he says!" he shouted at the soldier. "I've been waiting to light the Fire for twenty years!"

He let all his anger out by screaming.

He silenced and patted his clothes neatly and stood straight. He turned over and walked out.

The soldier said "Let The Fire Burn! Sir!"

The man shouted in anger " I want it done NOW." And went away.

CHAPTER 14

I woke from my sleep. It was still dark outside. I got up from my bed and looked out the window behind the bed. I was still in Heave. The city was in the darkness of the early morning. Houses were still asleep.

The trial was over. Hax, me, Drianne, Elliot and Bea survived. We went on to the final trial.

I can't get rid of the picture of Hax standing in front of me, when he made it on the trail.

It was like a light side I knew of him was going away

and the dark side came into picture.

As I looked out I saw a person on a horse. They were moving fast. The horse galloped to the gate as quickly as possible. The person wore a red cloak which flowed with the wind.

Red cloak.

I knew who they were. But what business at this time. I had already seen them out at night once. But now, twice.

Dia?

What is she doing here, now? More secret letter stuff?

Just yesterday I questioned her on how Hax and she were friends. But I didn't get a clear answer. Only side lines to distract me from the *truth*.

The truth.

Such a simple thing to ask but such hard to get.

Now, I need the truth from them. They've been hiding it for a long time.

From me.

I quickly put on my shirt missing a few buttons on the top and headed out the room. I stormed the halls trying to locate them.

As I reached the main hall, the big doors opened, silently. She came inside and removed her cloak and headed the opposite direction.

I silently followed her. In the same manner I did on that night. Taking turns along with her. She led me all the way to a small door on the wall.

It was small enough for her to enter. She went inside and shut the door. I walked to the door. Calmly opened the door and went inside.

I was behind a shelf of books and scrolls and other things. On the other side of the shelf I could hear Dia's footsteps.

I peeked through the books to see.

Secrets.

I saw Hax standing beside Dia. They were discussing it on

a desk. They faced away from me and a huge stained window lay in front of them. The moonlight was peering from the window.

Dia was panting and seemed to be in urgency. She handed over a letter to Hax.

Hax read it under his breath and his face turned to shock.

"Now!" he turned to Dia "Not now. We agreed after the Aztheon. They can't come."

Dia sighed "We can't do anything now. They're already at the gates. I came fast to inform you."

"All? Fifty thousand troops? Under whose authority?!"

Troops? What troops? What are they planning?

"Trickster. What should we do? What should we do, . . . about him?"

Hax seemed worried, more than ever. Beads of sweat rolled down his temple. He paced. Were they talking about me?

I need to know now.

I stepped in front of them and shouted "Hax!"

Dia shuffled to hide the matter. And Hax's worry increased.

"Azen."

"Who is the Trickster? Why are there fifty thousand troops outside the gates?!"

Hax stutured "It-It's not what you think Azen."

Enough of this, enough of these lies. "What are you hiding?!" I shouted.

"Calm down Azen."

Then the ground rumbled rhythmically. It sounded like an army marching very forward.

"They're here." Dia said.

Hax tried to explain "Listen–"

Then the sky outside the window turned red. Like flames. An ear bursting sound erupted. Like a volcano. The glass shattered, sending shards everywhere.

Everything was in slow motion. The two people

standing in front of me fell. I did too. Then the very brick wall came crumbling down, along with the roof.

I used my magic to stop most of the fall, but at last my vision turned dark and a faint ringing sound played in my ears.

And faded away. . . . Then a past vision appeared.

CHAPTER 15

I stood on a smooth hill. The grass was leveled and was waving to the wind. There was light fog all over. I could see Sols from here, at a distance through the fog.

I couldn't move nor speak. I was a mere spectator here.

Deja Vu.

I feel like I've been here before. Like I had a memory here. A certain emotional one.

Then I heard giggling coming from over the hill. I listened and waited for it. Two boys about ten years old came hopping my way.

One of them wore a black shirt with trousers and the other wore a brown vest over his white shirt.

They chased each other on the hill.

They reminded me of someone else. Someone I knew.

"Hax wait!" Said the one in the vest. I realised who they were. I tried to move but I couldn't.

They chased and passed me. I tuned to watch them still. They lay on the grass talking to each other.

Those were the days.

For a few minutes I watched them. They played and fought. THey walked over to the edge of a forest and decided to play there.

For a moment they enjoyed having company and played.

But suddenly a howl came from the forest. They boys stopped playing to listen.

"What was that?" I said. Hax replied "Wolves Dad told me all about them, come let's go see them."

Hax went into the forest and signaled me to follow. And I looked here and there into the forest. Trying to decide if I should go.

My face was fearful and I was scared. "Come!" Hax shouted from inside.

I kept watching myself. Then I moved slowly into the forest. Then with Hax we went to the sound of the wolves.

Hax ran fast, while I struggled to keep up. Each time they howled I was shook. At last I found Hax hiding behind a bush and peering through.

"Look, wolves." Hax whispered to me. I hid with him and watched.

There were five wolves all gathered around a dead deer. They were tearing it apart and eating it. Growls came from them trying to eat more.

The wolves fought for a greater share. Then a wolf who was a little bit small compared to the leader of the pack challenged the leader.

Growls and howls came from the two of them. With each sound my heart beat faster.

They fought horrendously. Rolling upon each other and biting, drawing blood.

Then the small wolf bit the other in the neck. With one snap the leader's face grew lifeless. Blood dripped from his wounds and he laid there.

Now, the small wolf was the leader, who will get more, more the share , and will grow stronger.

"They fight with the Alpha to gain dwominance." Hax said

while mispronouncing dominance.

"This act is like betrayal." Hax continued to explain.

Betrayal.

Then the vision disappeared, taking me back to the moment when I confronted Hax.

Hax stood there and said "Calm down Azen, It's only betrayal."

My heart beat faster, sweat rolled on my forehead. My once nice brother isn't so nice now.

Then I heard another blast awakening me from my dream . . . .

CHAPTER 16

"Hax?" I called out into the space. I didn't know where I was. But I could feel it. Heat grazed my skin. I could smell smoke.

Bit by bit my senses came to me. My eyes were covered. I was unable to see where I was. But, I could definitely tell there were fires around me.

Are they trying to kill me?

My brother, my own brother. It hurts so much. What could he be hiding from me?

Betrayal.

What was my subconscious trying to tell me? The wolves.

The alpha being betrayed by a wolf.

I need to know.

Just then my blind was removed. I was lying on the stone ground. My eyes adjusted to the fire light.

The fire surrounded . . . Sols. My country. My home was being destroyed before me.

Was all this Hax? Dia too?

"Hax! Where are you?" I shout asking him to show himself.

He walked out of the smoke, from the smoke of the fires he started.

He grabbed me and made me sit on a chair. I could see

the expression in his face after setting the city on fire.

He tied my hands and legs to the chair. As he did I asked "What is all this, why are you doing this?" He didn't answer.

"Tell me the truth!" I shout with tears lingering in my eyes.

He walks over and looks at me to tell.

"I'm not your brother." Hax said.

Eh?

I was stuck, not able to think. He must be lying, he must be joking.

"Tell the truth." I ask. "I'm not your brother. Well not biologically. I was born in Tricks. To my very dead parents. Who died in a fire. When Cortis destroyed Tricks". Hax explained.

Revenge.

The only practical reason why he is doing this. But one question still remained in my mind. Why did Father adopt Hax?

Adopt.

It is still hard to get over it. All these years it was kept a secret. We were brothers, but not in the real way.

"Why did Father . . . ?" I asked. The tears were still in my eyes lingering.

Hax walked to the back of me, and moved the chair closer to the center of the non lit area.

The chair creaked and scratched the floor. The fires were still active, eating away Sols.

The smoke was filling the area . As I breathed my lungs filled with the smoke. I struggled to breath properly and coughed.

"Trouble breathing.?" Hax asked.

That . .

He's doing this for fun. The nice side I knew of him is gone. His evil has been unearthed.

"You psycho!" I shout. Trying to get myself free of the chair. "You're doing this for fun. An eye for an eye? You've gone crazy. It's not our fault. The tricks attacked first."

"Your fault? You've always treated me like this. You and Dad- that excuse for a father. You've always treated me like an outsider." Hax said while walking in front of me.

Outsider?

"We've done nothing but treat you like our own." I shout, now the tears burst out.

"Ridiculous. Father always cared more about you. Made you involve with the kingdom more." He paused and looked me straight in my eyes.

"YOU always mattered more." Hax finally let out his pain. His pain of being left out.

It was true father did work me towards the kingdom. But, he too loved Hax.

He walked away facing away.

"Stop! Let me out!" I shout for his answer. I try to get free of the ropes. But in doing so I fall over to the side.

I see him walking away into the smoke. The world was turned sideways for me.

"Goodbye . . . brother," Hax said faintly.

Minute by minute the fires grew, drawing ever so closer. The smoke filled like fog. The dense fluid filled my lungs making my brain have no oxygen.

I had no way of getting out. I didn't have my sword with me. My magic didn't respond at all.

My eyes spun and my vision was snapping. At last my body gave out.

I can't . . . I am going to die

As my vision disappeared, I heard footsteps. Then they picked me up.

I tried to see who it was. I tried, then my eyes opened for a short time. I only viewed their blurry face. But, I knew who it was. The brown hair and the scar. It was the same person I saved . . . .

My life is not over yet. . .

Azen's story continues
in THE BROKEN

AUTHOR"S NOTE

I want to let you all know that this is my very first book. So, I ask all of you to be kind to me. I hope that this book has been an okayish experience for you. Because it would mean a lot to me, due to the months of effort I put in. I also wish this the first book in one of many. Thank you for reading till the end.

I extend my gratitude to my family, especially my sister for making me laugh while I work. I also thank Praneel, my friend for putting up with my banter about this book and supporting me.

And most of all I thank Y. Akilesh. One of my friends and an author who inspired me to write.

www.ingramcontent.com/pod-product-compliance
Lightning Source LLC
Chambersburg PA
CBHW021203130726
47988CB00002B/496